EXTREME ADVENTURES

CROCODILE ATTACK

This can't be happening! my slow-motion mind started saying to me, but I told it to shut up. This *was* happening. We *weren't* in a movie. That four metre crocodile swimming towards us *wasn't* a computer-generated special effect. It was real.

'Stay behind me,' I said to Nissa, and picked up the buffalo bone.

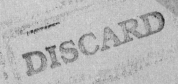

Puffin Books

Also by Justin D'Ath

Extreme Adventures:
Bushfire Rescue

Shædow Master
Infamous
Astrid Spark, Fixologist
Echidna Mania
Koala Fever
The Upside-down Girl

EXTREME ADVENTURES

CROCODILE ATTACK

JUSTIN D'ATH

Puffin Books

For Deacon

PUFFIN BOOKS

Published by the Penguin Group
Penguin Group (Australia)
250 Camberwell Road, Camberwell, Victoria 3124, Australia
(a division of Pearson Australia Group Pty Ltd)
Penguin Group (USA) Inc.
375 Hudson Street, New York, New York 10014, USA
Penguin Group (Canada)
90 Eglinton Avenue East, Suite 700, Toronto, ON M4P 2Y3, Canada
(a division of Pearson Penguin Canada Inc.)
Penguin Books Ltd
80 Strand, London WC2R 0RL, England
Penguin Ireland
25 St Stephen's Green, Dublin 2, Ireland
(a division of Penguin Books Ltd)
Penguin Books India Pvt Ltd
11, Community Centre, Panchsheel Park, New Delhi-110 017, India
Penguin Group (NZ)
Cnr Airborne and Rosedale Roads, Albany, Auckland, New Zealand
(a division of Pearson New Zealand Ltd)
Penguin Books (South Africa) (Pty) Ltd
24 Sturdee Avenue, Rosebank, Johannesburg 2196, South Africa

Penguin Books Ltd, Registered Offices: 80 Strand, London WC2R 0RL, England

First published by Penguin Group (Australia), a division of
Pearson Australia Group Pty Ltd, 2005

1 3 5 7 9 10 8 6 4 2

Text copyright © Justin D'Ath 2005

Text and cover design by David Altheim © Penguin Group (Australia)
Cover image by Sam Hadley
Typeset in ITC Officina Sans Book by Post Pre-press Group
Printed and bound in Australia by McPherson's Printing Group

National Library of Australia
Cataloguing-in-Publication data:

D'Ath, Justin.
Crocodile attack

ISBN 0 14 330223 X.

1. Crocodiles – Juvenile fiction. 2. Kidnapping – Juvenile fiction.
I. Title. (Series: Extreme adventures).

A823.3

www.puffin.com.au

1

BANG BANG, YOU'RE DEAD

Black beanie, dark blue raincoat, wet leather boots. A truckie, I thought as we passed each other near the meat and vegetables freezer. Nobody else would be out on a day like this. Two hundred and thirty millimetres of rain had fallen since lunchtime yesterday, according to Auntie Erin behind the counter. The wind was so strong I'd had to get off my bike at the roundabout and push it all the way up Main Street.

Nissa, my two-year-old cousin, was playing with some Space Rangers figures in the Kiddy Corner at the front of the general store. Sometimes Auntie Erin brought her to work if Mum couldn't look after her, or if the creche was closed. Mum had the flu that day and didn't want Nissa exposed to it. I'd fought my way to the general store to buy her some cough lollies. Apart from Auntie Erin's shop, everything was closed on account of Tropical Cyclone Kandy, a hundred and fifty kilometres offshore and headed down the coast.

I paused near the door to look at the latest issue of *Outback Survival* magazine. Nissa said something, but it was difficult to hear above the noise of the rain, hammering on the verandah's iron roof.

'What was that, Niss?'

'Bang!' she said, pointing a stubby finger like a Space Ranger's ray-gun towards the rear of the building.

I raised a pretend ray-gun of my own and turned to see where the aliens were.

At first I didn't understand what my eyes were telling me. The man in the blue raincoat was leaning over the counter. He seemed to be deep in conversation with Auntie Erin. The safe where she kept the banking records gaped open. While the man talked softly to her, Auntie Erin was busy filling a brown paper bag. With money!

2

The man noticed me gawking. 'Hey kid,' he called. 'Come here.'

He was holding something. It looked like two joined pipes with holes in the ends, roughly the size of ten-cent coins. I lowered my hand, all thoughts of Space Rangers forgotten. My mind was working in slow-motion. *That can't be a shotgun!* it told me.

'Are you deaf?' snarled the man. 'I said come here.'

My legs moved. Like a person in a dream, I walked towards the man with the shotgun.

This isn't real, my mind was saying. *Armed hold-ups only happen down South. In big cities. Not in friendly little towns like Crocodile Bridge.*

'I've only got some change,' I stammered, reaching inside my jacket.

The man shook his head. He was about as old as my big brother Nathan. He had a row of silver rings in each earlobe and a red goatee beard. 'Keep your hands where I can see them,' he said, 'and get down on the floor. You too,' he told Auntie Erin, taking the bag of money and stuffing it inside his dripping raincoat.

Auntie Erin and I lay face down on the floor. It still

didn't seem real. I felt like an actor in a Hollywood movie as the man with the shotgun stepped over us. He grabbed the wall phone and ripped out the cord.

'Don't even think of calling the cops,' he warned.

I listened to his boots creaking across the lino towards the front of the shop. I could no longer see him. Auntie Erin was blocking my line of vision.

'Man got bang-bang!' piped up Nissa.

'Bang bang, you're dead,' said the robber.

Auntie Erin lifted her head. 'Don't point that thing at my daughter!'

'I wasn't pointing it at her, lady. Now lie down like I –'

A siren interrupted him. For a few moments, we listened to the eerie wail in the distance.

'I *said* don't call the cops!' the robber shouted.

I heard scuffling from the front of the shop. Then Nissa squealed. Beside me, Auntie Erin scrambled to her feet.

'Leave her alone!' she cried.

Now that Auntie Erin was standing up, I could see what was happening. The robber held Nissa in the crook of his left arm. He was edging backwards towards the

4

door, the shotgun pointing at Auntie Erin.

'I said don't call the cops,' he repeated.

'How could I have called the police?' Auntie Erin pleaded. 'You disconnected the phone. That's a cyclone warning. Please put down my daughter.'

He shook his head. His eyes narrowed. 'Don't come any closer!' he warned.

'Please!' Auntie Erin begged. *'Please don't hurt her!'*

The robber nearly dropped Nissa as he wrenched open the door. A flurry of wind and misty raindrops swirled into the shop. 'If you want your kid back,' he yelled over his shoulder, 'tell the cops not to follow me!'

The door slammed shut and they were gone.

Auntie Erin let out a strange, low moan. She staggered sideways. A sunglasses display crashed to the floor. The glasses scattered around me. I jumped up and grabbed my aunt before she fell. She leaned heavily against me. A pair of sunglasses crunched under one of my sneakers as I helped Auntie Erin to a chair beside the counter. She buried her face in her hands.

'No, no, no, no!' she sobbed. 'He's taken her. He's taken my baby!'

I don't know what came over me. I am not the kind of person who acts without thinking something through. But before my mind registered what I was doing, I dashed out into the howling wind and rain.

2
HOSTAGE

The street was deserted. No people, no cars. Everyone was indoors, sitting out the cyclone watch in the comfort of their warm, dry homes. Only now it was a cyclone warning, if Auntie Erin was right about the siren. I should be inside, too. What did I think I was doing?

I ran to the corner of Arafura Street. Nothing there. A gust of wind blew back my jacket hood. The raindrops felt like bullets. They stung my face and ears. They nearly blinded me. I turned my back and the wind pushed me as I ran the other way. Back past the general store, with its Community Bank Agency sign lying on the footpath beside my fallen-over bicycle, through the flooded gutter and across Kakadu Lane.

Hang on! What was that?

I backtracked, my heart thudding in my chest as I peered cautiously around the corner.

There they were. Thirty metres down the laneway. A pale blue ute was parked half on the footpath. The passenger door hung open. The robber stood calf-deep in the overflowing gutter, struggling with Nissa, trying to push her inside. Nissa fought and kicked and screamed. Her hair was plastered to her scalp and her pink overalls were saturated. The shotgun lay on the vehicle's roof, raindrops dancing around it.

I splashed towards them. It still felt like I was in a movie. In my mind, I saw the brave young hero grab the shotgun and rescue the little girl, but the robber obviously hadn't read the script. He came wading towards me and positioned himself between me and the shotgun. He practically threw Nissa into my arms.

'Here, see if you can control the brat,' he said, wringing his left hand. It had a red, crescent-shaped mark between the thumb and forefinger. 'Watch out, she bites.'

Nissa was too panicked to realise who I was. She kicked and twisted and thumped the back of her head against my chest. She was soaked and slippery as a catfish. Finally, I managed to pin her arms.

'Calm down, Nissa,' I gasped. 'It's me. It's Sam. I'm the good guy.'

She looked up at me, her face red and streaked with rain and tears. 'Want Mummy!' she squeaked.

I hugged her. 'Shhh. It's going to be okay.'

The robber had retrieved the shotgun from the roof of the ute. He waved it at the open passenger door. 'Get in the car, good guy. And don't try anything smart.'

'I won't give you any trouble,' I promised. 'But you don't need both of us. Let Nissa go.'

The siren was louder now, rising and falling as it carried on the wind. He seemed to be listening to it.

'It isn't the cops,' I said. 'It's a cyclone siren.'

The robber levelled the shotgun at me. 'Shut your mouth and get in the car. Both of you. And keep the kid under control.'

I obeyed him, feeling numb. Part of me still couldn't believe that this was happening. *We're not being taken hostage!* it was saying, even as the man ran around the front of the ute and jumped in behind the wheel next to me. *It's just a dream or something.*

The robber gunned the ute out of the lane and turned left on Main Street. He shot down the hill, doing twice the legal speed limit. The road was wet and slippery. The ute nearly spun out of control on the roundabout. I held Nissa tightly. She was soaking wet and shivering.

We went right past my house. Dad was in Darwin for a conference, but Mum and the twins were home. *Look out the window, someone!* I prayed. The storm-blinds were down. Even if someone did look out, what would they see? An unfamiliar blue ute zooming by in the rain. Southerners, they'd think. Nobody else would be dumb enough to be driving directly into an approaching cyclone.

I was hoping the robber might let us out at the edge of town, but he showed no sign of slowing. The ute was doing over a hundred when Big Barry loomed into view.

The robber gave a low whistle. 'Man, would you look at the size of that!'

I said nothing. When you see something every day you take it for granted. Big Barry was the town's most famous landmark – a thirty-five metre fibreglass crocodile. As we crossed the bridge beneath him, I was looking down at the river. It was nearly flowing over the roadway. I had never seen it so high.

Only a fool would be leaving town on a day like this.

With trembling hands, I passed the seatbelt around Nissa and myself, and clicked the buckle into place. At last it sank in. This wasn't a dream. And it no longer felt like a movie. It was real. A robber had taken us hostage.

3
TOO YOUNG TO DIE

DRY SEASON ROAD ONLY, the sign said.

'You can't go down there,' I told the kidnapper.

He ignored me. Hardly slowing down to take the forty-five degree turn, he swerved off the bitumen. Nissa squealed in fright. I braced my legs and steadied her in my arms. The ute slewed left, then right, then left again on the rutted, water-washed road. As soon as we were going in a straight line again, the man's eyes flicked up to the rear-vision mirror. He had been doing this since we left town. I twisted round in my seat, bringing Nissa partway round with me. She looked up, eyes wide with fear. I smiled to reassure her. All I could see out the rear window was a brown rooster-tail of water thrown up by the wheels.

'Nobody's following us,' I said to the man.

'You heard the sirens,' he muttered.

'I told you, it was a cyclone warning,' I said. 'Haven't you been listening to the radio? There's a cyclone coming. We're driving right into it.'

He glanced sideways. 'Know something, kid? I don't like the sound of your voice.'

I don't like the sound of yours, either, I almost replied, but I didn't want to antagonise him. If his driving was anything to go by, he was nine parts crazy on a scale of ten. I didn't want to push him over the edge.

The road was narrow and bordered on both sides by gyrating, wind-whipped trees. The occasional wet-looking termite mound shot by as well. With all the rain we'd had in the past twenty hours, it looked more like a river than a road. I didn't want to think about rivers. I knew there was a real one ahead: Crocodile River. The same river we had crossed on the way out of town, only on this road there wasn't a bridge to cross it.

Whoosh! The ute hit a puddle the size of a cricket

13

pitch, throwing up a spray of mud that all but blacked-out the side windows. It bounced and swayed and slid. This was insane. I held Nissa tight. She was shivering again.

'We'll be okay, Nissa,' I said, wishing I could believe it.

'Want Mummy,' she murmured.

'I'll get you back to your mummy, I promise.'

'Bad man make Mummy cry.'

'Stop talking, you two!' growled the kidnapper.

I swivelled my eyes sideways. The shotgun was balanced across his knees. Both his hands gripped the steering wheel. If I was quick, I could grab the gun before he had time to react.

I dismissed the idea as soon as I thought of it. He wasn't much bigger than me, but he was an adult and probably much stronger. I was only fourteen, too young to die.

'There's a river along here somewhere,' I said nervously.

The robber gave no indication that he'd heard. He swung the ute sharply to avoid two half-grown wild pigs.

They charged through the mud- and water-filled canal that stretched ahead. The road had disappeared.

I moistened my lips. 'It's the same river we crossed before, but there isn't a –'

'Are you deaf?' he snapped. His right hand dropped from the steering wheel and wrapped itself around the rain-beaded stock of the shotgun. 'One more word, good guy, and I might have to shut you up. Permanently.'

As if you aren't going to kill us anyway, the way you're driving, I thought.

The windscreen wipers were set on maximum. They slashed back and forth across the rainwashed glass faster than the runaway beat of my heart. But they made little difference to the visibility. It was like driving through a car wash. I glanced at the speedometer. One hundred and thirty-five kilometres per hour. On this road! In these conditions! He was going to kill us, no question.

A yellow road sign flashed by. It was impossible to read at the speed we were going. But it's a sign that anyone who lives north of the Tropic of Capricorn sees every day. I didn't have to read it to know what it said. CAUTION FLOODWAY.

I couldn't keep silent any longer. At the top of my voice, I yelled: *'SLOW DOWN, YOU STUPID IDIOT!'*

The ute swooped over a low rise. My stomach climbed up into my ribcage as the road fell away beneath us. Nissa let out a piercing shriek. I might have cried out too, or maybe my scream was inside my head. Ahead, the landscape was on the move. For as far as the eye could see, a vast tract of brown floodwater churned and boiled directly across our path.

The robber hit the brakes. He was much too late. We went into a long, heart-stopping skid.

This is it, I thought. *This is the end.*

As the flooded river rushed towards us, I had time to squeeze Nissa in a protective bear-hug and brace myself for the impact.

WHUUUUMP!

A fan of spray exploded around us. Nissa and I were thrown forward against the seatbelt. Water in a wide brown wave rolled across the bonnet and up over the windscreen. Day turned to night. I knew my life was over.

4

TRAPPED!

Silence. Stillness.

Am I alive? I asked myself. *Or am I dead?*

There was no pain, just the racing thump-thump-thump of my heart.

Alive then, I decided.

I opened my eyes. It was very dark. The windscreen wipers were still working. Beyond them a wall of brown pressed against the glass.

The silence made no sense. What had happened to the rain? Where was the sky? The trees? The road?

Then it dawned on me. We were underwater. The ute was sitting on the bottom of Crocodile River and we were inside it. Trapped. We would never get out! Why had I interfered? I should have minded my own business. I should have let the robber take Nissa. What had I achieved by acting like a hero? Absolutely nothing. Now both of us were going to die. Now there would be two grieving families back in Crocodile Bridge, instead of one.

Suddenly the brown water peeled back and a strip of grey daylight opened along the top of the windscreen. Once again there was the sound of heavy rain on the roof; only this time it wasn't noise, it was sweet music to my ears. The ute had risen to the surface. It was floating.

I took a deep breath to calm myself. I knew I needed to be calm. I needed to think clearly. A ute wouldn't float in a river for long. I had to get out. I had to get out and back to shore. Get Nissa back to shore. Perhaps I could be a hero after all.

'Nissa?' I whispered to the top of her small, wet head. 'Nissa, are you okay?'

She didn't answer. Her body felt limp and cold and lifeless on my lap. She wasn't shivering any more. *Oh, please, don't let her be dead!* I prayed as I searched desperately for a heartbeat.

Nissa giggled. 'Don't tickle!' she said.

'Sorry.' I was so relieved she was alive that I almost giggled myself. 'Are you okay?' I asked.

'Big plash.'

'Yes. Very big splash.'

'Too much water,' Nissa said solemnly. She frowned at the big raindrops that flowered across the narrow strip of clear glass along the top of the windscreen.

'Way too much water,' I agreed.

It was like being in a submarine. Muddy brown, swirling with silt and debris, the floodwater pressed against the windows. Only the small strip of bluish-grey daylight around the top showed we were partially floating. In front, the windscreen wipers arced to and fro, their rubber strips catching and stuttering on the submerged glass as they fought to hold back the river.

A tremor ran through the ute. There was a loud scraping noise, then a tall reddish-brown column slid slowly past my window. It was a submerged termite mound. We were moving, being pushed along by the current. Being carried downstream. I wondered how far it was to the ocean. Part of me knew we would never get that far. The ute would sink long before that. It would settle on the bottom and that would be the end.

A cold sensation around my toes caused me to look down. My feet were underwater.

'Nissa,' I said, my voice high and unsteady, 'we have to get out of here.'

The cab was slowly filling with muddy brown water. Already the floor was covered. It was deeper under the dashboard because the ute was tilted forward at a slight angle. I could see a steady brown trickle coming in around the edge of the door near my left calf. A floating five dollar note and two soaked twenties nudged against my ankles. For the first time since we'd ploughed into the river, I turned to look at the robber. He was slumped forward with his head on the steering wheel. He hadn't been wearing his seatbelt. A small spider-web pattern blossomed in the glass directly above his head. Fat drops of pearly brown water seeped in through the net of fine cracks that radiated from its centre.

'Excuse me,' I said softly. 'Mister? Are you okay?'

He didn't respond. Didn't move. The shotgun was partially afloat under the dashboard between his knees. Just its cut-off wooden handgrip poked above the rippling surface. I carefully unclipped my seatbelt, shifted Nissa onto my left thigh, and leaned over, but I couldn't reach the gun without moving the robber's left arm out of the way. Afraid to touch him, I pulled my hand back.

'Bad man go nigh nigh,' Nissa said.

The ute swayed. A submerged tree trunk slid past my window, travelling from the back of the vehicle to the front. We had turned around since we passed the termite mound. Now our leaky submarine was facing upstream. The floodwater was carrying it along backwards. I don't know why, but this seemed worse than going forwards. I shut my eyes and leaned my head back in the seat. All at once I felt defeated. It was hopeless. We were never going to get out of this.

'Tam,' said a little voice. That was Nissa-speak for Sam.

'What?'

'Go home now?'

I remembered the promise I had made to Nissa earlier. *Me and my big mouth,* I thought. We were going to die, and there was nothing I could do about it.

But I had to try. I owed it to Nissa to at least *try* to fulfil my promise. Opening my eyes, I lifted the soaked, shivering little girl and turned her around to face me. I forced myself to smile.

'Guess what?' I said brightly. 'We're going for a swim.'

'No want wim,' she said.

'Nissa, it's the only way we're going to get out of here.'

She shook her head. 'NO WANT WIM!'

I sighed. 'Okay. I can probably carry you.'

First we had to get out of the ute. There wasn't much time. The cab was filling fast. If I opened the doors, floodwaters would rush in and send us straight to the bottom. We might even drown before we got out. I wasn't sure what to do. I needed an adult's advice. Gingerly gripping the robber's shoulder, I gave him a gentle shake.

'Excuse me. Can you hear me?'

He didn't answer. I dragged him clear of the steering wheel and pushed him back in his seat. He was heavy. His head slumped forward, his bearded chin resting on his chest. His beanie had come off in the crash and there was a large purple and red lump on his forehead. It looked pretty bad. Was it bad enough to kill him? I raised my voice to make myself heard above the loud hammering of the rain above our heads.

'Can you hear me?' I repeated.

Nothing. I shook the lifeless man again, roughly this time. I was getting angry with him. This was all his fault. Who did he think he was, coming to Crocodile Bridge and robbing Auntie Erin's shop, then kidnapping Nissa and me and driving at full speed into a raging flood?

'Wake up.' I shouted, jerking his shoulder savagely. 'Wake up, dammit.'

Thump! The noise seemed to come from behind. It was accompanied by a heavy jolt. The rear of the ute lifted sharply, tipping me forward in my seat. I braced my legs and grabbed Nissa to stop her from falling against the dashboard. For a few seconds we clung to each other, then she began to whimper.

'It's okay, Niss,' I said, knowing that it wasn't.

What had happened? We weren't moving. The ute tilted forward at a much steeper angle than before. Flood-water filled the whole windscreen now; even the strip of daylight along the top had disappeared. Yet the interior wasn't as dark as it had been when we'd first run into the river, when we'd been completely submerged. And I could still hear the rain on the roof.

I twisted around in my seat. Yes! The window at the back of the cab was completely above water. Beyond the rain-spattered glass, the ute's tray reared up against whirling treetops and scudding grey clouds.

Trees. We had run aground. We were saved!

5

'NAKE'

We were still trapped inside the ute. It was three quarters submerged in the swirling floodwater. It wouldn't be safe to open the doors. Our only escape was to climb out through the rear window. I had to work out a way to get it open.

There was one obvious solution. I leaned over the robber and grasped the shotgun's wooden stock. It was heavier than I'd expected. Two streams of brown water poured out of the barrels as I lifted it over the lifeless man's knees. Knocked out, he was no longer scary.

'Bang-bang,' Nissa snivelled.

'That's right,' I told her. '*Big* bang. Cover your ears.'

I knew a bit about shotguns because my brother Nathan owned one. He had taken me clay-target shooting once. But this wasn't like his gun. It was more like a very big pistol. I held it with both hands, pointed it at the centre of the rear window, and squeezed the trigger.

Nothing happened.

What was wrong?

Water was still leaking in around the doors. It was almost up to my waist. I was sitting in it. I could feel Nissa shivering as she clung to me. Perhaps the shotgun wasn't loaded. Fumbling, my fingers shaking and clumsy, I worked the lever that clicked the gun open. It was loaded, all right: there was a big, brass-backed shell in each barrel. I hoped water hadn't got in and wet the gunpowder. Closing the weapon, I tried to remember what Nathan had done. Safety catch, I remembered. Was this it? I pushed the little red button forward. Then I pointed the gun at the window again, clenched my eyes shut, and pulled the trigger.

The blast was deafening, and the force nearly jerked the gun out of my hands. Glass exploded everywhere. Nissa shrieked and clamped her arms around my neck.

'It's okay, Niss,' I said, my ears ringing. I gently freed myself from her stranglehold. 'Sorry about the noise.'

Wind and rain blew in my face. I used the smoking gun to chip the remaining glass shards out of the rubber seal around the edge of the broken window. Then I tossed the ugly weapon out into the ute's tray and turned to my little cousin.

'I'm going to lift you out,' I said, 'then I'll climb out after you.'

Nissa shook her head. Her face was red and tears dribbled from the corners of her eyes. 'Too much water!' she said, her mind made up.

I had learned that it was no use arguing with a two-year-old. 'Okay, I'll go out first.'

I wriggled out though the narrow aperture into the back of the ute. The forward part of the tray was half full of muddy water. Wind and rain lashed my face as I scrambled on hands and knees up to the tailgate. My heart fell. I'd been expecting to see land. Instead my eyes were greeted by a churning brown sea that stretched into the rain-blanketed distance. Apart from the occasional treetop and termite mound, everything was submerged. The trees I'd glimpsed through the back window stood in two or three metres of rushing water.

The ute had run aground on a very large termite mound. Wedged beneath the tailgate, its broad summit had been damaged by the impact. Gradually, the floodwaters were eating into the porous red clay. As I watched, a large chunk broke off and tumbled away in the frothing current. The ute trembled and seemed to subside slightly beneath me. We might be carried off at any moment.

I slid back down the tray. Nissa stood on the passenger seat, tummy deep in brown water. She raised her arms as I leaned in to lift her out.

'Bad man waked up,' she said in my ear.

Only then did I notice that the robber had turned his head slightly. His glazed, bloodshot eyes stared into mine from a distance of less than thirty centimetres.

'Help!' he gasped. 'Help . . . me.'

I was too shocked to say anything. I whisked Nissa out and carried her to the rear of the tray, where I sat her in one corner with her back to the tailgate. Removing my jacket, I wrapped it tightly around her.

'Stay here,' I told her. 'I'll be back in a minute.'

'Want Mummy,' she said, putting her thumb in her mouth.

I touched her cheek. I almost said, *I'll take you back to Mummy soon*, but stopped myself in time. No more rash promises.

The shotgun lay halfway down the tray where I'd thrown it. I made sure the safety catch was on, then I peered cautiously into the cab. I was careful not to point the gun directly at the injured man.

'Can you move?' I asked.

'Can't move my legs,' he said weakly.

I knew that was bad. 'Are you in pain?' I asked, remembering my First Aid from school.

'My head hurts.'

'What about your legs?'

The man shook his head. 'Can't feel them,' he said. 'Help me. Please.'

The water lapped around his chest. It swirled with half-submerged bank notes: fives, tens, twenties, even a fifty. Part of me didn't want to help him. He was the cause of all this. He had robbed Auntie Erin, he'd kidnapped my little

29

cousin, he'd even threatened to kill me. My hand tightened around the shotgun.

'Promise you won't try anything?' I said.

He made a little blowing noise, halfway between a laugh and a sob. 'What . . . could I do? Mate, I can't even . . . move!'

So I was his mate now. No longer 'Good guy' or 'Kid'. I didn't trust him, but I had no choice: I couldn't leave him to drown. I placed the shotgun on the narrow ledge where the front of the tray met the cab. I wanted it to be within easy reach. Then I wormed my head and shoulders in through the narrow gap.

'I'm going to turn you around,' I said. 'Then I'll pull you out into the tray.'

There was very little room to manoeuvre, and without the use of his legs the man was heavy and awkward. He had partial use of his arms, though, and helped as much as he could. Pretty soon we had him turned around. I dragged him up into a kneeling position on the seat and got him to take some of his own weight by gripping the rubber lip of the window hole. Then I reached in and clasped him beneath the armpits. I was so close to him that I could feel his bristly beard against my ear.

'Okay,' I gasped. 'On the count of three, we'll drag you out. One, two –'

THUMP!

The ute lurched sideways. I knocked my cheekbone hard against the man's head. Behind me, Nissa shrieked. I let go of the robber, reversed out of the cab and twisted around to see what was happening.

We were in a tree! A dark wet mass of leaves and branches blocked out half the sky. They completely engulfed the tray. I couldn't even see Nissa. From somewhere within the tangle of rain-whipped foliage, she was screaming at the top of her lungs.

'I'm coming,' I yelled. 'Stay where you are.'

I had no idea what was going on. How did we end up in a tree? But my main concern was Nissa. She sounded terrified. Almost in a panic myself, I fought through the swaying tangle of foliage. There were too many branches. I managed to snap two or three, and then I came across one almost as thick as my arm. When I tried to bend it aside, the entire thicket slewed slowly around. I rocked

31

the branch experimentally, and the thicket rocked, too. A floating tree! Now I understood what had happened. The tree had been uprooted by the flood and carried downstream in the current until it came to rest against the ute.

I took a firm hold of the branch and cautiously leaned my weight against it. I didn't want to push too hard, or too quickly, in case I dislodged the ute from the crumbling termite mound that supported us. Gradually, centimetre by centimetre, the mountain of foliage began to move out into the floodwater. When it was nearly clear of the tray, the current took hold. Slowly the tree pivoted against the side of the ute and swung around. For the first time I saw its enormous swollen trunk. It was a bottle tree – a baobab. It went rocking down the flooded river like a strange leafy whale. Thirty metres downstream it became stuck in the branches of a partially submerged gumtree.

I grinned at Nissa. 'It was just a floating tree, Niss. Nothing to worry about.'

Huddled beneath my jacket, Nissa seemed mesmerised by something beside her. At first glance I thought it was a branch. Nissa removed her thumb from her mouth and, in a small voice, said:

'Nake.'

6
TOO SCARED TO MOVE

At nearly two metres long, the dark brown snake lay in an elongated S shape across the high part of the tray. Its small bullet-shaped head was centimetres from Nissa's tiny pink toes, where they poked out from beneath my jacket. The only sign that the snake was alive came from its intermittently flickering black, forked tongue.

'Nissa,' I said softly, 'stay very still.'

I didn't know much about snakes but this looked like a bad one. A king brown. Perhaps even a taipan. It must have fallen out of the floating baobab. On all fours, I inched my way up the wet, slippery tray towards it. Nathan reckons that snakes aren't usually dangerous, unless they're cornered or threatened. I hoped this one didn't feel either one of those things.

When I was about a metre and a half from Nissa and the snake, I cautiously rose to my feet. Bracing myself as best I could against the gusting wind and the stinging flurries of rain, I leaned forward and slowly extended my hands towards Nissa, making a bridge with my arms across the deadly S of the snake.

'I want you to stand up,' I said, 'really, really –'

I had been about to say 'really, really *slowly*' when she sprang up into my arms. As she jumped, my jacket fell away from her and landed on the snake. Startled, the reptile coiled out of the way in a quick, fluid slide and finished up with its head resting against my right sneaker.

I froze. Balanced precariously in the sloping tray, Nissa in my arms, the snake at my feet, I was literally too scared to move.

'*Bad* man!' Nissa said in my ear.

Bad snake would have been more appropriate, I thought. Not that the snake had actually done anything bad – yet – apart from being there. And being a snake.

'Bad man got bang-bang,' Nissa said.

That was when I noticed that she wasn't looking at the snake. Her eyes seemed to be directed past me. Towards the cab of the ute.

Uh oh! I thought.

Very slowly, so as not to provoke the snake, I turned my head. And saw, framed in the ute's rear window, the top half of the kidnapper's head. Lined up against his right eye was something that looked, at first glance, like two joined pipes, with holes in the ends roughly the size of ten-cent coins.

'Stay right where you are!' he said menacingly.

7

DON'T COME BACK!

'What are you going to do?' I asked.

'I want you . . . very very slowly . . . to raise your right foot,' the robber said. His voice was coming in gasps as he raised it to make himself heard above the howling wind.

'Are you crazy?' I shouted. 'It'll bite me if I move!'

'Not if you . . . do it slowly,' he called. His eyes were screwed up against the stinging wind-borne rain. The gun's barrels wobbled alarmingly. 'Just raise it . . . high enough . . . to give me a . . . clear shot.'

I wasn't sure which I feared more, the snake or the shotgun. But I had to do something, and soon. Nissa was growing heavy and it was almost impossible to balance in the gale-force wind. To make matters worse, I had noticed in the last few moments that the ute was moving slightly from side to side, as if it was about to break free from the termite mound.

'Just make sure you don't shoot me!' I cried.

And lifted my foot.

As soon as I moved, the snake reared up and struck. Clearly, terrifyingly, I saw its long curved fangs bury themselves into the toe of my sneaker.

I'd been bitten by a snake!

I lurched backwards, lost my balance, and toppled over the side. A skyful of heavy black clouds wheeled momentarily above me, then floodwaters closed over my head like a cold brown door.

Invisible currents tugged at my clothes. They spun me dizzyingly around. For a few panic-filled moments, I felt myself being swept away. Then my shoulder bumped against something solid. I made a blind grab. My fingers clutched metal. The strong current pushed me sideways, but I held on. I dragged myself to the surface and spat out a mouthful of water. One of the ute's tail-lights loomed above me. I was clinging to the exhaust pipe. Grabbing the bumper with my other hand, I pulled myself around behind the tailgate. Sheltered from the full force of the current by the ute's wide body, the water was calmer. My hip nudged against the submerged termite mound. By digging one foot into it, I was able to raise myself slightly in the water. I hooked my right hand over the top of the tailgate and hung there, gasping, trying to regain my breath.

Something moved in the brown water next to my shoulder. A small scaly head rose above the surface. The snake. It must have fallen out of the ute when I did. I suddenly remembered that it had bitten me. Already its deadly venom was working its way through my veins towards my heart. I would probably be dead within half an hour. But that didn't make me any less terrified as the evil-looking reptile flickered its forked tongue at me. Its head was centimetres from my nose. I was almost cross-eyed trying to keep it in focus. I couldn't move. I simply watched as the snake slid up onto the bumper and slithered across my bare left forearm. It felt like wet leather. Its scales rippled past my eyes. Now it reached my right arm, the one that gripped the tailgate. Instead of going over it, the snake wound underneath my right elbow and came up around the other side, high up near my wrist. It was long. About a metre of it still dangled over my left arm. I could feel its wide belly scales flexing against my skin. There were goose bumps running up and down my arms, and – I swear this is true – every hair on my head was standing straight up like needles. When the snake's head reached my right hand, it stopped, turned and looked down at me. Silhouetted against the roiling storm clouds, it flickered its tongue. Then it continued up across my hand and over the top of the tailgate into the tray.

About half a metre of it was still sliding up my arm. As its scaly black tail twirled past my eyes, I thought of Nissa. I had to keep the snake away from her! It had already bitten me, so what did I have to fear? You can only die once. Without really knowing what I was going to do, I wrapped my left hand around the tail. Quick as lightning, the part of the snake that was in the ute came looping out over the tailgate, doubling back on itself, its pink mouth wide open, striking at my face. But I was no longer scared. It was as if someone else was holding the snake, not me. With a flick of my wrist, I flung the reptile into the air. It sailed over my head, twisting against the low grey sky like a piece of rope, and splashed into the swirling water metres away.

'And don't come back!' I called after it.

I hauled myself over the tailgate and fell gasping into the sloping tray. The water inside the ute was level with the water outside now. The tray was awash. Almost the entire cab, including the lower half of the window opening, was submerged. The robber had managed to drag himself partway out, though his lower body and paralysed legs were still inside the cab. In one hand he held the shotgun.

'Where's the kid?' he asked.

The world stopped. I flicked my wet hair out of my eyes. The robber and I were the only people in the ute.

8
GONE

Scrambling to my knees, I scanned the raging floodwaters downstream of the ute. My heart hammered.

'*Nissa!*' I screamed, sudden tears blurring my vision. '*Nissaaaaaaaaaaa!*'

There was no answer, just the low mournful howl of the wind.

'Sorry, mate,' the robber said behind me. 'She's . . . gone.'

I turned on him. 'It's your fault!' I yelled. Sliding down the tray, I wrenched the shotgun from his grasp and hurled it into the roiling floodwaters. 'If it wasn't for you, she'd still be here!'

'I wasn't the one . . . who fell over the side . . . with the kid in my arms,' the injured man gasped.

'You made me lift my foot!'

'I was trying to . . . shoot the snake.'

'But you didn't shoot it, did you?' I cried.

'How could I shoot it?' he asked. 'It was . . . wrapped around your . . . shoe.'

I lifted my sneaker out of the rain-pocked water that slopped about in the tray. I wasn't in pain. Perhaps the fangs hadn't penetrated the reinforced rubber on the toe. I really didn't care. All I could think of was my cousin. Little Nissa. I'd promised to take her back to her mother. She had trusted me. Now she was *gone*. I would never see her again. It did not seem possible.

I sat on one of the wheel-arches and steadied myself against the side of the gently rocking ute. I sniffed back a tear. 'I must have just let her go.'

'It was an accident,' the man said, his words all but lost in the wind. He blinked the rain out of his eyes. 'Could you . . . help me . . . please? I don't feel . . . so . . . good.'

I glared at him. I wished he was the one who'd been

43

swept away. 'She'd still be alive if you hadn't kidnapped us.'

A strange expression crossed his face, a look halfway between surprise and fear. Then his eyelids fluttered closed and he collapsed.

'Hey,' I yelled. 'Are you okay?'

It was a stupid question. He was jackknifed through the narrow window, his ginger hair floating around his head in the water at the front of the tray. I grabbed his upper arms and lifted his face out of the water. His body was limp. It was like carrying a sack of cement. But somehow I managed to drag him out of the cab. I lay him on his back near the tailgate. The water was only a centimetre or two deep at this end. His eyes were still closed and his face was so pale it looked almost blue. It made the livid red and purple swelling on his forehead seem more shocking.

Using my body to shelter him from the lashing wind and rain, I searched one of his wrists for a pulse. After a few nervous moments, my fingertips detected a faint beat. My own heart pumped with relief. Much as I despised the robber, I didn't want him to die. I didn't want to be left alone in the middle of the river, with Cyclone Kandy bearing down on me.

Not that I expected either of us to live for much longer.

Wherever you are, Nissa, I thought, gazing up into the bruised sky, *I reckon I'll be joining you soon.*

9
THE WORST DECISION OF MY LIFE

The first time I heard it, I thought it was the cry of a waterbird. A jabiru, or a duck. I didn't know much about birdcalls, but the plaintive shrilling note, barely audible in the raging wind, sounded like a bird to me.

The robber opened his eyes. 'What was . . . that?'

'A bird,' I said. 'How are you feeling? You lost consciousness for a couple of minutes.'

He rolled his head one way, then the other. His bloodshot eyes settled on me. 'Where . . . am I?' he asked weakly.

I explained to him what had happened and how I had pulled him out of the cab.

'I guess I owe you,' he said. The cry came again and he frowned. 'That's a weird-sounding bird.'

He was right. There it came again, a high, strange sound. It sounded almost human.

Could it be . . . ?

I peered over the tailgate. The cry seemed to be coming from the direction of the floating baobab. It was still caught in the branches of the half-submerged gumtree thirty metres downstream.

Squinting through the rain, I thought I saw a movement. Yes! There it was again! Something small and white was waving among the clump of exposed roots. It looked like a tiny hand.

'Nissa!' I screamed.

I leapt to my feet and was nearly blown out of the ute.

'Hey, watch yourself,' growled the robber, reaching with one hand and dragging me back down into the tray.

'It's her,' I said, my skin prickling. 'It's Nissa. She's alive!'

'Where?' asked the robber. He rolled onto his stomach and dragged himself up to peer over the tailgate.

A slow smile broke over his face. 'Plucky little kid,' he said.

The current must have washed her under the baobab. She had caught hold of it somehow and climbed up among the roots. I began unlacing my sneakers.

'What are you doing?' asked the robber. He sounded worried.

I dragged off a sock. 'Going after her.'

'Are you crazy? You'll never make it.'

'Nissa made it,' I said. 'The tree's directly downstream. All I'll have to do is keep my head above water and the current will do the rest.'

'How will you . . . bring her back?'

'I'm not bringing her back.' I pulled off my other sock and studied my toes. There were no signs of punctured skin. The snake hadn't bitten me after all. 'I'll stay there with her.'

'What about me?' asked the robber, fear in his voice.

I couldn't look at him. 'You should be all right. The ute's stuck on a big termite mound. I don't think it'll move.'

We both knew I was lying.

Barefoot, I slid one leg over the tailgate.

'Please,' the robber said to my back. 'Please . . . don't leave me.'

'She's only two years old,' I said. 'She won't survive on her own.'

'Take me with you.'

I looked at the foaming water that tugged at my foot and ankle. I wished he hadn't asked. This was the man who, less than an hour ago, had pointed a shotgun at me and threatened to take my life. It would have been simpler if he had died when he cracked his head against the windscreen.

'I'm not a very good swimmer,' I said. 'We might both get sucked under.'

'I can help . . . stay afloat,' he said. 'My arms are . . . okay. I tell you what – if I start . . . dragging you down, you can let me go.'

I wondered if *he* would let *me* go. I've heard of drowning people dragging their would-be rescuers under and drowning *them* in their panic.

Just then a grinding noise came from below. The ute trembled and sank about five centimetres in the water.

'*Please!*' the robber begged.

I sighed. 'Okay.'

I hoped I hadn't made the worst – and last – decision of my life.

10

BAD MAN

Here goes nothing! I thought, and pushed out and away from the ute.

I had seen a lifesaving video once but had never actually tried carrying another person while swimming. You were supposed to swim on your back, dragging the disabled person behind you. It worked for about two seconds, then the current caught us. Everything became a whirl of clouds and spray and water. Once I glimpsed the rear of the ute fly past in the distance, another time the blurred top of a tree. Mounds of heaving brown water broke over us like ocean waves. There were coughs and grunts and loud choking gasps. Someone's hand clawed at the spinning sky overhead. We went under, came up, went under again. We were completely at the flood's mercy, as helpless as two socks in a washing machine. I knew we were going to drown.

It was the robber who saved us. If he hadn't reached out and grasped one of the baobab's branches, we would have been swept right past it. *He* was holding *me* now. He could have let me go, but he held grimly on and slowly dragged both of us in among the tree's trailing foliage. Finally, I managed to grab hold of a branch of my own. Then, side by side, floodwater churning over us, the robber and I hauled ourselves into the thicket of whipping, splashing leaves. Close to the grey wall of the baobab's trunk, I found a large, thick branch that projected out parallel to the water's roiling surface. I clambered up onto it. Using just his arms, and with a bit of help from me, the robber hauled himself up beside me. Our combined weight caused the tree to roll slightly, dipping us up to our thighs back into the floodwater. Above us, the baobab's trunk loomed against the sky like a wet stone wall. At the far end, a small pink-clad figure huddled in the shelter of the broken-off roots. She was sucking her thumb.

'Nissa!' I called.

She stood up uncertainly, gripping one of the up-flung roots for support.

'No, stay where you are!' I yelled, worried that the wind would blow her into the river. 'I'll come to you.'

It was easier said than done. The fat bottle-shaped trunk was smooth and slippery looking, and there were no branches for most of its length. I would have to crawl across, fully exposed to the gale, or else lower myself into the flood and drag myself along the waterline. Neither was possible if I was taking the robber with me. And I couldn't leave him on his own. The effort of getting this far seemed to have sapped his remaining strength. His eyelids were closing again, his head nodding.

'Hey. Are you okay?' I said.

He blinked, his eyes only half open. ' . . . sleepy,' he murmured.

'Stay awake!' I shouted. He was sliding back into the water. 'Don't go to sleep!' I yelled, grabbing hold of him.

It was no good. His eyes closed and he sagged against me, blacked out again by another spell of concussion.

I was stuck. There was nothing I could do but stay

with the unconscious man and support him until he regained consciousness. As long as the tree did not roll further, and as long as I held on, we would be safe. But I was worried about Nissa, crouched next to a big Y-shaped root at the other end of the baobab. She was wet and cold and scared. A picture of misery. My arms should have been wrapped around her, not around our kidnapper.

'Hey, Niss. How's it going?' I called. Only about four metres separated us, but I had to shout to make myself heard above the howling wind.

She said something that I didn't quite catch. I think she was asking when I was coming to get her.

'Soon,' I yelled. 'When the man wakes up.'

I almost said *bad man*, but I'm glad I didn't. It's true that he had got us into this mess. But a short while ago he had saved my life.

11

EMPTY FINGERS

I'm not sure how much time passed. My watch had stopped, and the robber wasn't wearing one. It felt like hours. The branch was not much thicker than a baseball bat. It dug into me. Soon I had lost all feeling in my backside and legs. A crocodile could have come along under the water and bitten off both my feet and I probably wouldn't have known about it until I started to pass out from loss of blood. I didn't think there was much danger of that happening. Even though it was called Crocodile River, and there *were* crocodiles in it, the bad ones – the salties – hardly ever came this far inland so early in the wet season. The water was normally much too low. All that had changed in the past twenty-four hours, but I doubted that crocodiles could swim upriver in the swift floodwater. It was amazing how fast the river was flowing, and how quickly it had risen.

I wondered how close Cyclone Kandy was. The heavy-bellied black clouds raced so low across the sky that it felt like I could touch them, and the wind seemed to be growing stronger by the minute. When a huge gust rocked the baobab and nearly blew Nissa off the top, I shouted at her to climb right in among the roots.

'Nitta frighted,' she whimpered.

'It's okay, Niss, I'm here,' I called.

She was only four metres away but there was nothing I could do to help. My hands were full. Literally. One was wrapped around the unconscious man, the other clung to a big branch above our heads. If I let go with either hand, one or both of us would be sucked away by the floodwater.

Nissa said something about a car.

'What was that?' I shouted.

'Car come,' she said, pointing.

For a moment I had a ridiculous thought. *They've sent*

a search party and found us! But when I looked through the screen of baobab leaves, all I saw was the ute. It had pivoted around on the termite mound and was facing us. Only its roof and the tip of the tailgate remained clear of the water. Nissa was right, though – it *was* coming in our direction. Slowly, centimetre by centimetre, the ute was sliding off the termite mound. With a final shudder, it broke free. I watched it come spinning towards us through the swift current, sinking as it came. In a few seconds it crossed the thirty metres between the termite mound and the baobab. It swept beneath us, a wide pale shape in the murky depths. There was a massive jolt and a cloud of bubbles erupted on the surface. Nissa screamed. I found myself falling backwards as a frenzy of branches came windmilling down out of the sky, plunging me into the flood.

I don't know how long I was underwater. It was probably only five or six seconds, but it seemed like fifteen minutes. I was tangled in a net of invisible branches, being pushed down and down and down. Then, miraculously, I was above water again. Being lifted up.

Later, I realised what had happened. The ute had

dislodged the baobab from the gumtree that had been holding it. Suddenly freed, the bloated trunk had swung out into the current and rolled like a performing seal. It had rolled through 180 degrees, its branches dragging me and the robber around with it. I didn't understand this at the time. All I knew was I'd been dunked beneath the surface and lifted out again.

The robber groaned. He coughed up water. We were both suspended in a hammock of branches a few centimetres above the flood. The baobab had stopped rolling. It was now swaying back and forth in the current, dipping us in and out of the water.

'What . . . happened?' he muttered.

'I'm not sure,' I gasped, relieved that he was conscious again. I gripped a branch and twisted myself around on the flimsy platform. A flurry of rain stung my eyes. The robber said something else but I didn't hear what it was. I was looking at the roots, which clutched at the sky like the hand of a drowning man.

Where was Nissa?

1 2
CHINA DOLL

I hauled myself up the side of the baobab, bawling. I didn't care if the robber heard me. In fact, I *wanted* him to hear.

'This is all your fault!' I shouted back at him. 'I hate you!'

Rain lashed my face, mixing with my angry tears. I was angry all right. Angry at the robber, angry at the cyclone, angry at the flood; I was even angry at the baobab for pitching Nissa into the water. Most of all I was angry at myself for allowing her to be taken by the flood a second time. I should have been with her. Instead of staying with the robber, I should have gone to Nissa. I should have looked after *her,* not him. He was the cause of all this.

I walked along the length of the baobab's trunk, standing upright. I think I only made it because I was so angry. It was as if, for the three or four seconds it took me to get from one end to the other, Cyclone Kandy was scared of me! Falling against the wet broken roots, I looked out over the flood.

Tree tops poked out here and there. Logs and debris rocked along in the current. A low hill moved past perhaps two hundred metres away through the teeming rain, but there was no sign of Nissa. I slumped forward, defeated.

Wait a minute, I suddenly thought. *These are different roots. Where's the big Y-shaped one that Nissa was sheltering under?*

That was when I worked out how the baobab had rolled 180 degrees, dragging the robber and me from one side to the other. But Nissa had been on top of the tree to begin with. If she had become caught in the roots and was dragged through 180 degrees, then she would be . . . *underneath it!*

I leapt into the flood. What I didn't realise at the time, and what saved me from being swept away, was that the baobab was no longer caught in the gumtree; it was being pushed along by the flood, and so was I. Relative to each other, the floating tree and I weren't moving. Jackknifing my body, I dived headfirst down beneath the splayed branch-like roots. I grabbed hold of one, then another. Hand over hand, I used the roots to pull myself down beneath the baobab. The water was brown and muddy. I couldn't see more than a metre in front, but I knew she was down there somewhere.

Nissa, I cried out to her in my mind. *I'm coming.*

We nearly bumped heads. Her small round face was centimetres from mine. Her eyes were wide open; she seemed to be looking at me. But her mouth was open, too, and no air was coming out. *Close your mouth*, I was thinking, fighting to free her. One of the shoulder straps of her pink overalls had become twisted around a root. I tried to rip it free but the root bent back and forth, resisting my efforts. The cloth of her overalls seemed to be made of denim; it wouldn't rip, either. I tried to find a button but there wasn't one – the strap was sewn into the garment's bib. The stitching was strong. I grabbed the strap in one hand and began working it along the root towards its broken-off end. The root was about a metre long and pointing down into the cloudy depths. It was hard to see what I was doing. One of Nissa's little hands waved lifelessly in front of my eyes. I had to push it out of the way several times. My lungs were bursting even though I had been under the water for a fraction of the time Nissa had. Her mouth was open. Her hair floated around her face. She seemed to be looking at me, but could she see anything out of those wide-open brown eyes? How long did it take to drown? The current tossed us back and forth. Leaves drifted slowly past. At last I reached the end of the root. With a final desperate heave, I pulled Nissa free. Holding her lifeless body in the crook of my left arm, I fought my way back towards the pale ceiling of daylight high above.

I broke through the surface with a huge gasping whoop. It was a close thing – two more seconds, I reckon, and I wouldn't have been able to hold my breath any longer. I was light-headed from lack of oxygen. There was a roaring in my ears. My limbs felt leaden. But there was no time to rest. I lifted Nissa's face clear of the water. Her lips were blue. She wasn't breathing. I had to get her up onto the baobab. There was no time to lose. Rain sizzled on the water as I worked the unconscious child close to the tree trunk where the roots were bigger and thicker. I climbed them like a ladder, dragging Nissa behind me. My breath sawed. She was surprisingly heavy. I hauled her up onto the swaying trunk and laid her in the shelter of the upflung roots. Her eyelashes fluttered but it was just the wind. Her eyes were firmly closed. Her skin was deathly white. She looked like a china doll.

She looked . . . *dead!*

I had never given anyone mouth-to-mouth resuscitation before. At First Aid classes we'd used a dummy called Oscar. He was twice as big as Nissa, even though he was just a head and half a plastic body. Nissa was so small! So lifeless! Tears smeared my vision as I knelt over her. I tried to recall what you were supposed to do. You didn't just tip the head back and start blowing.

Clear the airway, I remembered.

Gently, I opened Nissa's mouth and poked a finger in to check that there was nothing stuck in her throat.

And she bit me.

Then she spewed up about a litre of water, all over my hand and wrist. I rolled her onto her side and she coughed up an impossible amount of water. No wonder she'd felt so heavy.

Nissa opened her eyes and looked at me sideways. And both of us started bawling.

13

NATHAN

The robber had called Nissa a plucky little kid. He was right. No way could I have survived underwater for as long as Nissa had. She recovered quickly. I think she was the first to stop crying.

'Tam tad?' she asked.

I was sitting with my back to the roots and my arms wrapped tightly around her. I was never going to let her go.

'No, Niss, I'm not sad,' I snivelled. 'I'm happy.'

Crying because I was happy. How soppy is that? But it was true. Regardless of our situation, I *was* happy at that moment. Happy to have my little cousin back. Happy that she was alive. And happy, too, that I'd saved her. I knew it was a pretty brave thing I'd done. Pretty damn heroic, actually. I felt good about myself. Sam Fox, real-life hero!

But I didn't have long to enjoy the feeling. There was the robber to think of. I'd left him suspended on a flimsy support of branches centimetres above the flood. Now that Nissa was safe, I should go back and check on him. And, if possible, drag him up onto the baobab's trunk. It's what anyone would have done, I told myself.

Nissa wasn't happy about it. She clung to me and wouldn't let go. I had to pry her hands gently loose, one finger at a time.

'The man's sick, Niss,' I explained. 'I've got to go and help the sick man.'

'Bad man!' she said, and thrust her thumb into her mouth.

I persuaded her to nestle in among the roots. Not too far in – I didn't want her to get caught in them if the tree rolled again. I felt bad about leaving her, but I had no choice. The robber had saved my life, after all.

I crawled slowly out onto the slippery, rocking trunk. I

wasn't going to risk standing up this time; my anger had been replaced by relief, and with relief came caution. There was more than just my own life at stake now. If I fell off, Nissa would be left on her own, and I knew she wouldn't be able to survive without me. Neither would the robber.

I couldn't see him as I edged my way out onto the exposed tree trunk. That didn't bother me at first. There were lots of leaves and branches between us, and he was wearing dark clothes. But the closer I came to the leafy end of the tree, the more uneasy I became.

'Where are you?' I called.

There was no answer. I slithered down the last half metre of smooth wet bark and crouched in the fork of the tree's two main branches.

'Are you there?' I shouted. 'Hullo?'

The only reply was the mournful wail of the wind and the relentless slap of raindrops on leaves.

I called again, several times, then I struggled through the slippery foliage until I was directly above the platform of branches where I'd left him. The man was gone. He must have fallen unconscious and slipped down into the water.

Propping myself up as best I could in the branches, I peered over the raging floodwater. There was no sign of him.

'Hey!' I called.

That was when I realised I didn't even know his name. Eventually I would find out it was Nathan, the same as my brother's name. Nathan McDonald, twenty-three years old, unemployed factory worker. He'd had some bad luck and made some wrong choices, but even as I stared into the tumbling river I knew Nissa was wrong. Nathan McDonald wasn't a bad man. A bad man wouldn't have held onto me as we were swept past the baobab. A bad man would have let me go.

'Hey!' I screamed again. The turbulent water stretched away in all directions, like a vast inland sea. 'I just want you to know I came back for you!'

14

CYCLONE KANDY

The full force of the cyclone struck about twenty minutes later. It was like nothing I'd experienced before.
The wind must have reached two hundred kilometres per
hour. It made a deep, savage, howling roar that filled
the universe. Ribbons of lightning darted through the
low blue-black clouds. Thunder boomed. The whole
sky was on the move, racing overhead at an incred-
ible speed. Nissa and I huddled against the baobab's
roots and hung on for our lives. I sheltered her as best
I could with my body, and took the brunt of the storm
on my back. The raindrops felt like hail. My thick bush-
shirt provided no protection from the stinging attack.

I was pummelled by the wind. It was hard to hang on. Beneath us, the tree swayed and tipped and pitched. It was tossed around like a cork by the huge winds and the wild water. Every so often a wave broke over the trunk, a rushing wet wall that slammed me forward with the power of a rugby tackle. I was worried that Nissa would be squashed between me and the roots. Each time a wave hit, I arched my back against it and pushed out with my arms. Several times I bumped my head hard against the roots. I saw stars. I became dizzy and disorientated. My knees felt chafed and raw from sliding on the wet bark. The muscles in my arms screamed out for relief. But I couldn't let go. All I could do was hold on and pray that the cyclone would pass quickly. And that the baobab wouldn't roll again. If it did, that would be the end for us. There would be no climbing back onto the tree this time if we fell into the floodwater. Not even a Hollywood hero could have survived.

We were lucky. Later, I found out that the eye of the cyclone crossed the coast forty kilometres to the south. Only its outer perimeter passed over us. Cyclone Kandy made its way inland, gradually losing ferocity and turning into a rain-bearing depression that caused floods over much of the Top End.

Forty minutes passed. Or maybe it was an hour. It's hard to estimate time when your whole world is reduced to something resembling the inside of a kitchen blender. The wind died down. It happened with surprising suddenness: one moment it was howling, the next it wasn't. Just a slight breeze tickled the back of my neck. I no longer had to hold on for my life. It was still raining, but at least it was falling vertically now instead of horizontally. It no longer stung. The roar of thunder was fading into the distance. I remained kneeling where I was for a few more minutes, my numbed hands still gripping the roots. I was cold and dazed and exhausted, and probably suffering from shock. My forehead hurt where I'd knocked it against the tree.

'Tam?' said a little voice from beneath me.

Slowly, I relaxed my arms and leaned back. Nissa looked up at me, her face deathly pale, her eyes ringed with pink and blue stains of exhaustion.

'Tam take Nitta home now?' she asked.

I smiled, or tried to. My jaw felt stiff from being

clenched tightly closed. *No more rash promises*, I reminded myself.

'I don't know, Niss,' I whispered hoarsely. 'I'll do my best.'

That was when I noticed how still everything was. Not just the air, but the baobab as well. It was no longer pitching and swaying. It didn't seem to be moving at all.

Stiff and sore, I climbed shakily to my feet. I helped Nissa up too. Standing side by side on the high trunk, her tiny hand in mine, we gazed out at a sight more beautiful than anything I'd laid eyes on in my entire fourteen years, four months and sixteen days on this planet.

Land.

We were saved!

1 5

DON'T EVEN *THINK* CROCODILE!

The baobab had run aground in a patch of mangroves. Beyond them, a coconut palm rose high into the rain-filled sky, and behind that stood a few straggly gumtrees. Mangroves only grow in tidal water and coconuts aren't inland trees, which means we'd been swept nearly all the way to the coast. We must have been close to the river mouth. That explained the waves that had pummelled us at the height of the cyclone. Perhaps the tide had been in at that stage and now it was retreating. Behind me, out in the open water, the current looked strong. I could see logs and leafy branches and other unidentifi-able debris being carried past by the flood. I wondered if Nathan McDonald was out there somewhere.

I piggybacked Nissa down the ladder of roots and jumped with her into the water. It came up to my chest. Nissa was used to being wet now and hardly seemed bothered. She clung trustingly to me like a baby koala to its mother as I worked my way, half swimming, half climbing, from one mangrove to the next, all the way to dry land.

It wasn't dry, of course, but after our terrifying ordeal, anything that wasn't underwater looked pretty inviting. I waded through the ankle-deep sludge and collapsed on a patch of damp pebbly ground, Nissa beside me.

'We made it,' I gasped, letting the fat cool raindrops splatter my face. 'Nissa, we're on our way home.'

It proved to be another rash prediction.

Ten minutes later, when I recovered sufficiently to get up and explore, I made a grim discovery. We were on an island.

It wasn't a big island. Standing on a soft sandy mound at the island's highest point, I estimated it was no more than forty metres long by fifteen metres wide. Just a narrow spit of land in a sea of swiftly moving water.

Floodwater, not seawater, but I knew the sea was not far away. Straining to see through the teeming rain, I made out a hazy stretch of riverbank in the distance. The tops of several trees poked above the floodwater between it and the island. They grew almost in a line. If the current hadn't been so strong, it might have been possible to swim from one tree to the next all the way to shore. It was something to keep in mind for when the floodwaters receded. Provided a search party didn't find us first. In the meantime, there was nothing to do but wait.

Nissa pulled impatiently on my hand. 'Tam take Nitta home now?'

She must have thought I was Superman. I crouched next to her. 'The river's too high, Niss. We'll have to wait a while.'

Tears welled in her eyes. She wrapped her arms around my neck. 'Want Mummy,' she murmured.

'I know,' I said, lifting her. 'Let's go and find some shelter until this rain stops.'

Apart from the mangroves which ringed its shores – and which were mostly underwater anyway – there were only four trees on the island: the coconut palm and three skinny gumtrees. None offered shelter from the incessant rain. I turned a full circle on the mound. At the far end of the island was a low thicket. It wasn't big, but possibly we could crawl inside it and escape the worst of the weather. I carried Nissa down to investigate. As we drew near, I thought I heard a rustling noise; but there was no wind, so it might have been my imagination. Then I heard it again. I stopped.

The thicket was denser than I'd first thought. Growing along the base of a metre-high rock shelf, it was a tangle of bushes and palm fronds and what looked like driftwood, all stitched together with some kind of a leafy vine. The rock shelf projected slightly over the heavy foliage; it was impossible to see into the dark space beneath.

'Hullo?' I said, feeling foolish. If anything was in there it would be an animal of some kind. Or more likely a bird. What kind of animal would live on a tiny island like this?

Don't even think crocodile, I told myself.

Raindrops pattered around us. There was no other sound. I strained my eyes into the thicket. Probably nothing was in there. I was exhausted and my imagination was playing tricks on me.

One of the palm fronds wobbled. So did my heart.

'Tam . . . ?' said Nissa.

'Shhh,' I whispered.

I lifted her from my right hip to my left. A bone lay half buried in the sand next to my foot. It was huge. It must have been the leg bone from a buffalo. Giving no thought to how the buffalo came to be there, or how it died, I stooped and dragged the heavy bone out of the wet sand. Then I took a deep breath and pitched it into the thicket.

Nothing much happened. There was the swish of the bone passing through the outer layer of leaves, followed by a soft thud as it hit something solid, then the only sound was the patter of raindrops. Slowly, I let out my breath. False alarm. There was nothing in there.

A twig snapped.

A vine twanged.

Uh-oh! I thought, and took half a step backwards. But it was too late to turn. Too late to run.

A large dark shape exploded out of the thicket like a

train out of a tunnel. All I was able to focus on as the creature charged was its pink slimy snout, its small narrow eyes and its yellowed, razor-sharp tusks. A wild boar!

I managed to leap out of the way. Almost. As it hurtled past, the huge boar struck me a glancing blow with its bristly flank, pitching me to the ground. Nissa landed on top of me. Terrified, expecting another attack, I rolled onto my knees and launched Nissa up onto the rock shelf. Then I scrambled up after her, all in the same movement. Only then did I look around. Halfway down the island the boar was still running. It seemed as intent on escaping from us as I was from it.

Nissa was crying. The palms of both her hands had been grazed on the rock when I pushed her up.

'Bad Tam!' she spluttered.

I was bad? I had just saved her from what was possibly the biggest, meanest, ugliest wild boar in the entire outback, and this was all the thanks I received?

Still, the poor kid had been through a lot in the past few hours. She was plucky, all right. One at a time, I raised her pudgy little hands to my lips and softly kissed their scraped palms.

'All better,' I said.

I was relieved when Nissa rewarded me with a small quivering smile.

16
THE NEXT THREAT

Nissa removed her thumb from her mouth. 'Nitta hungry,' she said.

We were huddled in the thicket, partway under the rocky overhang. It was cramped and smelled strongly of wild pig, but it was dry. Only in the past hour or two, since we'd found shelter and our lives were no longer in danger (or so I thought), had hunger become an issue. Neither of us had eaten since breakfast, which seemed like half a lifetime ago but was probably no more than twelve hours.

'I'll find something to eat in the morning,' I said.

This wasn't another rash promise. There was a coconut

palm, so there would probably be coconuts. But I wasn't searching for them tonight. Our clothes were beginning to dry and I didn't want to go out into the rain again. It felt wonderful to finally be almost dry. Besides, it was nearly dark and I was worried about the wild boar. He was somewhere on the island and I didn't want to run into him in the dark.

I had been thinking a lot about the wild boar during the past couple of hours. How had he come to be on the island? Had he, like us, been swept here by the flood? Or had he swum across from the riverbank? Then I remembered the line of trees between the island and the shore. It dawned on me that this wasn't an island at all, but merely part of the riverbank that had become cut off when Crocodile River flooded. The wild boar had *walked* here! That meant he could walk back, and so could we. All we had to do was wait for the floodwaters to recede. Once I worked this out, I cheered up and was almost able to ignore my growling stomach. But Nissa kept reminding me.

'Nitta hungry.'

'Go to sleep.'

'Tam get coconut.'

I had been silly enough to mention the coconuts earlier. 'In the morning,' I said, rocking her gently like Mum used to do when I was little. 'Go to sleep.'

'Nitta hungry!'

Mum used to sing to me too, but I wasn't about to do that. Besides, I'd just remembered something. The cough lollies. I could feel them, a soft lump in the back pocket of my shorts. The soggy cardboard fell apart as I pulled out the box, but the lollies seemed dry inside the plastic wrapping. I gave one to Nissa and popped another in my mouth.

'Have a lolly,' I said.

Nissa chewed a couple of times, then screwed up her face and spat out the pink soggy mess. 'Yucky,' she whimpered, starting to cry.

They *were* a bit hot, I realised. I sucked on mine for two or three minutes, until the worst of the sting was gone, then popped the soft jelly into Nissa's mouth. She stopped crying and began chewing. She didn't seem to mind that the cough lolly was second-hand. We shared the rest of them like that: I chewed the heat out of them, then Nissa ate what was left. It wasn't much of a meal, but it was better than nothing. By the time we'd eaten the last of the cough lollies, night had fallen. It was pitch black; I couldn't see a thing. Nissa relaxed into my shoulder and fell asleep.

I was feeling sleepy too. It had been a very long day – the longest, scariest, most eventful day of my life. As I cast my mind back over everything that had happened, my thoughts kept returning to the ginger-bearded robber, the man who had started it all. The last thing I said to him before he'd been swept away was 'I hate you!' I hoped he hadn't heard that. If it had been possible to save both him *and* Nissa, I would have.

I stayed awake for as long as I could – keeping guard, or so I told myself. When we first took over the pig's lair, I had retrieved the big buffalo bone and placed it within easy reach. My plan was to use it like a club if the boar, or anything else, came visiting during the night.

Little did I know how useless it would be against the next threat we'd have to face.

17
JUST IN CASE

In the dream I was back in the ute. It had just plummeted into the river and the cabin was filling with water. It came up to my waist. Nissa was poking me in the nose and shouting.

I woke up.

Nissa *was* poking me in the nose. She *was* shouting.

'Tam, Tam!' she was crying. 'Water come!'

I pushed her hand away before she poked out my eyes. I was still half asleep, but I was alert enough to realise that I was no longer dreaming. I wished I *was* still dreaming. Because, as well as Nissa's poking and shouting, there was another part of the dream that seemed to have followed me out of the land of sleep.

I *was* up to my waist in water!

My mind raced in circles. How could we be back in the ute? We'd *escaped*. I tried to stand up and knocked my head hard on the underside of the rock shelf. The pain woke me up fully and, finally, I remembered where we were. On an island. In a thicket. And somehow there was water in the thicket. Then it dawned on me.

The river was still rising.

'Come on, we've got to get out of here,' I said to Nissa.

I felt above my head where the rock shelf ended and broke a hole through the tangle of vines and foliage. I lifted Nissa out onto the rock and climbed after her. We were out of the water now. I could see it below us; or, rather, I could see the reflections of stars dancing on its black rippling surface.

Stars? I thought, and looked up.

The sky was clear. It was no longer raining. I had no idea when the rain had stopped, nor what time it was. I estimated that the river had risen nearly a metre since we'd crawled into the thicket. The shoreline had been ten or twelve metres away then, now it lapped around our feet.

I stood up and looked in the opposite direction. Dimly, I could make out the other end of the island; it seemed to be no more than twenty metres away. The island had shrunk. It was only half the size it had been yesterday afternoon. If the river rose another metre, I realised with a shock, the island would be completely submerged. Just as well the rain had stopped.

Nissa tugged on the hem of my shorts. 'Piggy come,' she whispered.

I could see it now: a dark silhouette beneath one of the skinny gumtrees. Only a dozen paces separated us. I lifted Nissa onto my hip. The boar didn't seem to be moving. It had run away from us yesterday. We were probably safe so long as we remained calm and didn't antagonise it.

'Nice piggy,' I said softly, hoping my tone would show it that we meant no harm.

'*Bad* piggy!' said Nissa, in a tone that conveyed the opposite.

The boar gave a little snort. It turned and ambled off

towards the other end of the island. So much for all the stories my brother Nathan used to tell me about how dangerous they were. But I wasn't completely reassured. Placing Nissa on the rock, I stepped down into the bushes and felt around with my feet in the water until I found the bone. *Just in case*, I thought, leading Nissa to the base of the gumtree where the pig had been. We settled down to wait for daylight.

18
WHERE PIGGY?

Once again I'd been having dreams about being stuck in the ute. And once again I awakened to find water lapping around my feet and lower legs. It was still very dark. Beside me I could see Nissa's small form curled up on the ground. The water hadn't reached her yet. I picked her up and gently carried her a few metres further along. The poor kid was so exhausted, she didn't wake up. There wasn't much of the island left now. It was only about ten metres from one end to the other, and roughly half that distance across. The boar stood six or seven metres away, a large black silhouette against the water at the far end.

'That's a good fella,' I said. 'You stay there and we'll stay here.'

It was a stand-off. The boar had one end of the island and we had the other. Would that still be the case if the river continued to rise? Keeping one eye on the animal, I backed down to the water's edge and stooped to pick up the buffalo bone.

The moment I lowered my head, there was a tremendous splashing noise at the other end of the island. I raced back to Nissa and stood over her, holding the heavy bone like a club in front of me. The splashing continued for a few seconds, then subsided into an eerie silence. My skin prickled. My heart raced. I peered into the darkness, turning my eyes right and left. There was no sign of the boar. I even looked behind me but it wasn't there. The animal had disappeared. I picked up Nissa and carried her onto the mound at the island's highest point. As I placed her gently down on a bed of sand and leaves, her eyes opened.

'Where piggy?' she asked.

'Piggy swam back to shore,' I told her. And hoped with all my heart that was true.

19

'YIZARDS'

I didn't get a moment's sleep after the boar disappeared. For what must have been two or three hours I sat nearly motionless, holding Nissa and staring over the black expanse of water. Gradually, the water crept closer. And closer. By the time dawn spread its first pink glow across the sky, the mound was all that remained of the island. It was two metres in diameter and half a metre high. Everything else, apart from the tops of the three gumtrees and three quarters of the coconut palm, had disappeared beneath the floodwater. Even the baobab tree, which I now regretted leaving, had been swept away.

'Nitta hungry.'

I looked down at her and tried to smile. I hadn't realised she was awake. 'I'm sorry, Niss. There's nothing to eat.'

She struggled off my lap and stood up. I stood up too. My legs felt wobbly and my feet sank a few centimetres into the unstable mixture of sand and rotting leaves that composed our tiny island. Nissa took hold of my hand.

'Want go home now,' she said, determined.

'I know,' I said. 'So do I.'

My eyes searched the sky. If a helicopter was going to come looking for us, now would be a good time. The horizon remained empty for a full 360 degrees. There was land to either side, but it was a long way off. The line of trees between the island and the shore had vanished overnight, submerged beneath the rising water. I remembered how the wild boar had disappeared and my skin prickled. Deep down I suspected what might have happened, but I didn't want to think about it. Fate, however, was working against me.

'Yizard,' said Nissa.

'Beg your pardon?' I asked, not taking much interest.

She released my hand and crouched down for a closer

91

inspection of something on the ground. 'Cute baby yizard,' she said.

I heard a strange chirping sound and suddenly I *was* taking interest.

'Get back!' I cried, grabbing Nissa by the shoulder and roughly pulling her away. 'Don't touch it!'

Nissa was right: it *was* a baby and it *did* look cute. But it wasn't a baby lizard. It was a baby crocodile. I recognised the sound it was making from a documentary I'd seen on TV. It was calling its mother!

The baby crocodile was only about fifteen centimetres long, but I wasn't taking any chances with those needle-sharp teeth. Lifting it by the tail, I tossed the little reptile out into the swirling water.

'Go find your mum,' I called as it wriggled away across the surface. 'And don't bring her back here, okay?'

I felt something move beneath my bare foot and stepped quickly to one side. From the deep sand- and leaf-lined foot mark, a little reptilian head looked up and chirped.

'Nother yizard,' Nissa cried happily.

I was anything *but* happy. I noticed a small movement

behind her. A clump of sandy leaves shook, then fell to one side as a third reptile appeared. Then a fourth. Now I understood what was going on.

Our tiny island, the squashy mound where Nissa and I had been forced to take refuge, was a crocodile's nest! Buried in the sand and rotting vegetation beneath us was a whole stack of crocodile eggs.

Perhaps it was the floodwater. Perhaps it was us stomping over them, or maybe they had been due to hatch anyway. Whatever caused it, the eggs started to hatch at that moment, and it was very bad luck for Nissa and me. Because as each new-born crocodile dug to the surface, it joined its voice to that of its siblings, making a high-pitched yelping chorus that no mother crocodile could ignore.

Nissa tapped me on the arm. 'Tam.'

'What?' I said, busy scooping up baby crocodiles and pitching them into the river.

'Yizard come.'

'I know.'

'Big yizard,' she said.

I straightened up and turned around.

This can't be happening! my slow-motion mind started saying, but I told it to shut up. This *was* happening. We *weren't* in a movie. That four-metre crocodile swimming towards us *wasn't* a computer-generated special effect. It was real.

'Stay behind me,' I said to Nissa, and picked up the buffalo bone.

20
CROCODILE ATTACK

I expected it to come in a rush. I'd seen crocodiles on TV, and when they attack they generally hit their victims at about one hundred kilometres per hour. But this crocodile was a mother, and she didn't want to trample her babies.

She climbed slowly up onto the mound, making a low growling sound in her throat and nudging the little crocodiles aside with her broad, scaly snout. I backed down into the water on the other side, waving the buffalo bone in the giant reptile's face, and keeping Nissa behind me. The nearest of the three gumtrees rose out of the rippling water about five metres away. Our only chance was to get to it before the crocodile got to us. Against all hope,

I prayed that she would stop when she had reclaimed her nest, when we'd been driven off the mound and no longer posed a threat to her babies. But she kept coming. Over the top of the nest and down the other side. Backing slowly away from her, I was nearly knee-deep in the water. Nissa was immersed up to her waist. Her thumb was in her mouth, and with her other hand she clutched the hem of my shorts.

It was now or never. If the crocodile reached the water before Nissa and I reached the tree, we'd be dead meat. Literally. I had to stop her now, while she was still on the mound. I also knew, deep in my heart, that I didn't have a chance.

Maybe, just maybe, I could delay the huge creature long enough to get Nissa to the tree.

'Go to the tree, Niss,' I said over my shoulder. 'Run!'

She can't run to the tree. The water's too deep, some logical part of my brain told me, but I was through listening. If I was going to die, I didn't want it to be in vain. I didn't want everything we'd been through in the past twenty hours to be for nothing. Nissa had to survive!

With a despairing cry, I launched myself at the crocodile, swinging the buffalo bone with all the strength I had. 'YAAAAH!'

As I rushed forwards, so did the crocodile. She took me by surprise and spoiled my aim – made it better, as things turned out. Instead of hitting her on the nose as I'd intended, I gave the crocodile a solid whack between the eyes. Momentarily stunned, she tilted her head to one side and snapped blindly at the source of the attack. I whipped my hand out of the way, releasing the bone. It was a hundred to one chance: somehow the crocodile's mouth closed over the makeshift club, end-to-end, and the bone lodged there, wedging her jaws wide open. She went into a frenzy, roaring like a lion and swinging her head frantically from side to side. I leapt out of the way but I wasn't fast enough. The crocodile struck a massive blow across my thighs, sending me flying.

I landed in the water three metres away. For a few moments there was no feeling. My body and my mind were numb. Floating peacefully on my back, I became dimly aware of a commotion nearby – a tremendous roaring and splashing. It made no sense. I didn't know where I was.

Something gripped my arm. Then a small pale face framed by rattails of thin blonde hair thrust itself between me and the peach-coloured morning sky.

'Tam!' it said. 'Tam, get up!'

Everything came back in a rush. The peaceful feeling disappeared, to be replaced by mortal fear. I splashed to my feet. It was agony. My legs felt as if a car had run into them. But that was the least of my concerns. Five or six metres away, the crocodile was roaring as it thrashed and twisted and rolled over and over in the water, throwing curtains of spray fully ten metres into the air. At any moment it might dislodge the bone from its jaws. And then there would be trouble.

I lifted Nissa onto my hip and waded, limping painfully, to the tree. The trunk was barely thicker than my arm but it was our only hope. It divided into a fork just above my head. Standing waist-deep in the eddying floodwater, I pushed Nissa up into the narrow V and told her to climb onto a small nearly horizontal branch about a half metre above that. Nissa didn't seem to understand. She clung to the fork and wouldn't move. She was looking over my head, in the direction of the crocodile's nest.

All at once I became aware of the silence. There was no more roaring and splashing. All I could hear was the rasp of my own ragged breath. Too scared to look behind me, I gripped the fork just above Nissa's hunched shoulders, wrapped my legs around the skinny trunk and hauled myself partway up the tree. But Nissa was in the way. I couldn't climb any further without squashing her. Hanging there with my dripping backside centimetres above the water, unable to go up, and too scared to go down, I risked a quick peek over my shoulder.

As I'd feared, the crocodile had dislodged the bone from her mouth. Fortunately for me, she seemed to have forgotten who was responsible for putting it there in the first place. Instead of coming to get her revenge, she was climbing ponderously back up the nest. Her babies – there must have been twenty now – were gathering around her, squawking excitedly as they wiggled and wobbled towards her fearsome toothy jaws. Then the crocodile did something that nearly made me fall out of the tree. She snapped her head sideways and ate one of the newly-hatched babies! In the next instant – snap! snap! – she had eaten two more.

I had heard that crocodiles were cannibals, but watching it was kind of gross. I wasn't too upset, though. As far as I was concerned, it was better that she ate her babies than Nissa and me.

My arms were trembling from the strain of holding onto the branch, and my bruised legs were killing me. I lowered myself back into the water, and moved around behind the tree trunk. It was too narrow to hide behind, so I crouched down until only my head was above water, making myself as inconspicuous as possible. With any luck, the crocodile would forget I was there and swim away as soon as it had eaten the last of its babies.

'Bad yizard!' Nissa said loudly, from the tree above my head.

'Shhh,' I whispered.

Too late. The damage was done. The crocodile had heard us. It turned its massive head and gazed directly at me. As we eyed each other across five metres of water,

I knew I was next on the menu. I had nowhere to go. I couldn't climb the tree, and the nearest dry land was more than a hundred metres away. I was dead meat.

Then a strange thing happened. As the crocodile lay there with its jaws partly open – drooling, I imagined – one of the remaining babies climbed into her mouth and wriggled out of view.

Huh? I thought.

Then I noticed something even more weird: a row of little eyes peeping out between the adult's teeth. The babies were alive in there! The big crocodile *wasn't* eating them, she was rescuing them from the rising floodwater.

I watched, fascinated and relieved, as she took the rest of her brood carefully into her mouth. I was relieved because I had worked out something else, something very significant to my present situation. If the mother crocodile's mouth was full of her babies, it was highly unlikely that she would want me in there as well.

What I hadn't worked out, and what was even more significant to Nissa and me, was another reason why mother crocodiles sometimes carry their babies around in their mouths. It's to protect them.

From other crocodiles.

21
DEATH-ROLL

At first I hardly noticed the log. Over the past eighteen or twenty hours I'd seen many logs floating in the river. Besides, when you're crouched in the water only five metres from a fully grown saltwater crocodile, you don't take much interest in the scenery. But the mother crocodile did. As the log slid slowly past the nest, she raised herself high on her front legs and sent a growling hiss in its direction. All the babies in her mouth stood up on *their* front legs and, poking their tiny heads out through the gaps between their mother's enormous teeth, they hissed too. I looked at the log again, and realised it was going the wrong way. It was moving against the current, coming *up*river – towards me.

And it wasn't a log.

I thought the mother crocodile was big, but this one dwarfed her. It was a male, a bull crocodile. I could tell by its size. Its head must have been nearly a metre across. The monster rushed at me. And its mouth, when it opened wide, looked as big as a bathtub.

It came so fast that there was no time to move. I couldn't have moved anyway – I was paralysed, resigned to my fate. But the bull crocodile wasn't after me. It wasn't even aware of my presence as I cowered behind the tree. Its eyes were on Nissa. When it reached the tree, it launched itself upwards, its massive head and shoulders rearing up like a tyrannosaurus rex. I didn't see any more; I was flung back by the impact of two tonnes of voracious reptile hitting the other side of the skinny tree. As the tea-coloured water closed over my head, I saw a huge shadow looming above me and heard a high-pitched scream, then the gunshot crunch of the monster's jaws slamming shut.

Assuming Nissa was dead, I simply let myself go limp. It would be better to drown than to be caught in those horrendous jaws and spun round and round in a death-roll that would wring the life out of me like water out of a twisted sheet.

The human body won't let itself drown when there's air close by. Besides, the water was little more than a metre deep. Next thing I knew, my head was poking above the surface. I began breathing again, softly, because the bull crocodile's scaly body was circling past, so close I could have touched it. It had no idea I was there. It was looking up into the tree, where Nissa – alive! unscathed! – was looking down, her body rigid with fear. Even though *I* hadn't been able to make her climb higher than the first fork, the monster crocodile had managed to persuade her to scramble up to the next branch.

'Tam make bad yizard go way?' she whimpered.

I would have liked nothing better than make it go away. But how? I no longer had the buffalo bone, and even if I did, I doubted whether I could pull off that stunt again. Not in the water. Not against a crocodile of this size. It looked easily six metres long.

'Tam get Nitta down?' she asked.

I gave her a tiny shake of my head. She was safe up there, relatively safe, anyway. Safe compared to me. Very slowly, with only my eyes and nose above water, I backed away from the tree and from the scaly monster circling beneath it.

'Tam!' Nissa cried. *'Tam!* Don't go way!'

I knew I couldn't say anything without alerting the bull crocodile to my presence. And I certainly couldn't stay where I was. As I backed away, the female crocodile watched me from her nesting mound. I was no longer worried about her – she had her babies to look after. But I wondered what she, a mother, would think of me for abandoning Nissa, for ignoring my little cousin's cries.

I had no choice; there was nothing I could do other than try to stay alive.

The further away I moved from the tree, the deeper the water became. Increasingly, I had to hold myself against the current. My bruised shins hurt from the constant straining. I would never make it if I tried to swim ashore. My only chance was to get to one of the other trees. The palm tree was the closest. The top towered fifteen metres above the flood. If I could reach that, and maybe climb it, I might be able hang on until a rescue helicopter arrived.

If a rescue helicopter arrived. Would they know to search in the river? As far as anyone knew, the robber had taken the coast road. If the search was taking place, it might be centred several hundred kilometres to the south.

'*Tam!*' Nissa shrilled.

I looked in her direction and my heart lurched. What was she *doing*? She had climbed back down into the lowest fork! Now she was less than a metre above the water. The bull crocodile could reach her easily if it made another lunge.

I raised my head slightly and looked around. Where *was* the monster? There was no sign of it. For just a moment, my spirits rose. Maybe it had given up and gone away. We were safe!

Then I saw something that shattered my hopes. Fifteen metres from the tree, a swirl dimpled the current. Two yellow eyes broke the surface, followed by a long horny snout. Further back, a double row of tall saw-toothed scales appeared, dragging a swift V-shaped ripple that moved arrow-like towards Nissa's dangling legs.

I stood up, head and shoulders out of the water, and yelled, '*CLIMB BACK UP!*'

Nissa looked at me but didn't move.

'NISSA, CLIMB UP!' I screamed. The bull crocodile was less than five metres from the tree and increasing its speed. 'GO HIGHER!'

It was too late. Nissa still hadn't moved. Even if she moved now, she could not get out of the way in time. The monster was sliding through the water like a torpedo. It was massive, unstoppable, a killing machine. Nissa didn't have a chance.

Part of me didn't want to look. But I couldn't stop myself. Nissa and I had been through so much together. By closing my eyes, I'd be denying my responsibility, I'd be turning my back on her. There was nothing I could do for her now. She was going to die, no matter what I did. I couldn't simply shut my eyes and pretend it wasn't happening. I had to watch. I had to be with my little cousin in her final moments.

Plucky kid, the robber had called her. She wasn't even screaming.

As the crocodile reached the tree, I flinched. My whole body cringed as if it was me, not Nissa, being attacked. But I forced my eyes to remain open, forced myself to watch. A big sob was already rising in my chest.

Take me! I wanted to yell out to the horrible creature. *Take me instead of her!*

The crocodile passed directly beneath Nissa's bare feet and shot out the other side. It swung in a smooth wide arc and came weaving straight towards me.

I looked into its evil yellow eyes with their strange slit pupils. I watched the two lines of tall pointed scales that trailed behind them. I felt numb. This was what I had asked for – my life instead of Nissa's – but now that it was about to happen, I knew it wasn't what I'd wanted at all. People shouldn't be given choices like that. I *wasn't* a hero. I didn't want to die, and I especially didn't want to be killed by a crocodile.

But it was too late. There was no escape. I was as good as dead.

22

'BIIIIIIG YIZARD'

I closed my eyes. I did not feel obliged to watch my own death. Every muscle in my body was tense as I waited for the horrific impact of the monster's jaws.

Nothing happened.

That's not quite true. *Something* happened, but not what I'd expected. Instead of being hit by the crocodile, I was hit by its bow-wave. The force was enough to make me lose my precarious balance in the swiftly flowing river and I was washed off my feet. My head went underwater. Still expecting to be struck at any moment, I held my breath and allowed the current to carry me along. Finally, after five or six of the longest, most suspense-filled seconds I'd ever experienced, there was an impact. But it wasn't from the crocodile. It was from being swept into the trunk of a tree. I instinctively clutched it and raised my head above the water.

Nissa's feet dangled a few centimetres above my eyes. Her small concerned face, wet hair plastered to her fore-head, looked down at me.

'Biiiig yizard,' she said solemnly.

The big lizard was on my mind, too. Somehow it had missed me, but it would not make the same mistake twice. Leaping to my feet, I grabbed hold of the forked trunk on either side of Nissa. This time, fired by the adrenalin of my close encounter, I hauled myself up past her without a problem and clambered onto the skinny branch above her head. Then I dragged her up after me. The whole tree swayed precariously. But as long as it didn't snap we would be okay. Provided the river didn't rise any higher, bringing us into the bull crocodile's reach.

What had happened to it? I searched the water below us. There was no sign of the huge reptile. I thought it was strange that it hadn't followed through with its attack. I'd been a sitting target, an easy meal, yet the creature had swerved away at the last moment, knocking me off my feet with its wash. It was almost as if it had lost its nerve.

Or, as if something had scared it away.

'Big yizard,' Nissa repeated, her small damp body wedged against mine.

'Yes,' I said, shivering and dripping, but happy all the same. (At least, as happy as you can be when stuck in a tree on a submerged island in the middle of a flooded river, teeming with saltwater crocodiles.) 'But it's gone now.'

It seemed too good to be true. The female crocodile had disappeared as well. The nest, or what remained of it, was empty.

'Big yizard come,' Nissa said, pointing behind me.

Uh-oh.

I twisted round to look. And nearly fell out of the tree.

No wonder the other crocodiles had left. This one was GINORMOUS! Its mouth, which was wide open, could have swallowed both of them. At the same time! From a crocodile this size, the tree offered no refuge at all.

I tensed as the giant came steadily towards us. I firmed my grip around Nissa. With my other hand, I clung to the branch above me. My knuckles were white. My bruised leg muscles quivered, my toes were spread and bent like a monkey's. I knew I'd have to get my timing exactly right.

At the last moment, when the monster crocodile was about to hit the tree, I leaned away from the trunk, let go of the branch, and jumped into its mouth.

23
ABANDON CROCODILE

I learned afterwards what had happened. The flood didn't reach my home town Crocodile Bridge because it's on a hill. The swollen river swept away the bridge after which the town is named, and with the bridge went our world-famous landmark, the thirty-five-metre fibreglass crocodile, affectionately known as Big Barry.

Somewhere on his seventy kilometre journey down Crocodile River, Big Barry became separated from the rest of the disintegrating bridge. Because he was hollow and water-tight, he floated over or around every obstacle, all the way to the coast. The island where Nissa and I were stranded was nearly at the end of Big Barry's journey. And it would have been the end of ours had he not shown up when he did.

Nissa and I rode in Big Barry's cavernous mouth for the final kilometre and a half to the coast. The water grew increasingly choppy as we came nearer to the sea. We got seasick, but neither of us had anything left in our stomachs to spew up. It made me worry about what lay ahead. The sea, waves. Sharks. Where would we end up, I wondered, provided we didn't get pitched into the surf and eaten, or stung by box jellyfish, or drowned? Would Big Barry float all the way to New Guinea? Or would he float aimlessly in the open sea while Nissa and I slowly starved or died of dehydration?

Or would a rescue helicopter find us and whisk us away to safety?

I liked the idea of the rescue helicopter, but I *didn't* like the idea of waiting to be rescued when I knew it might never happen. That's why I saw the railway bridge as our last chance.

The bridge spans the mouth of Crocodile River and is built on tall concrete pylons to withstand the high tropical tides. It was undamaged by the flood and cleared the water by a good four metres as Big Barry passed beneath it on the way out to sea. Big Barry was riding three metres above the water at his highest point, which was the tip of his wide-open upper jaw. That's where Nissa and I balanced, awaiting our chance to abandon ship (or abandon crocodile, to be more accurate).

The bridge was concrete; there was not much to grip onto. I had been hoping to scramble onto it, holding Nissa; now I could see that was impossible. I needed both hands to haul myself up, but I couldn't do that while holding Nissa. As we passed under the bridge, I lifted Nissa as high as I could and pushed her onto the bridge's smooth concrete span. By the time she was up there, Big Barry had floated too far under the bridge for me leap up after her. I had to duck down and wait for him to float out the other side, then grab hold of the bridge in the split second before Big Barry was out of reach.

It was a close thing. I just managed to hook my fingers over the concrete edge before Big Barry drifted away and left me dangling. I hung onto the smooth, powdery concrete by my fingertips. My legs swung in empty air. My arms felt like rubber and I couldn't haul myself up. My fingers were slipping. I looked around desperately. There was nothing else to grab hold of, no way up over the hard concrete lip. I was considering letting go and allowing myself to fall back into the river, then making an attempt to swim for it, when Nissa appeared over the edge. Wet and dishevelled, she looked down at me with her big, blue-ringed eyes.

'Tam take Nitta home now?' she asked.

She probably saved my life. I don't think I'd have been able to muster the strength to climb up onto the bridge if she hadn't been waiting for me. Depending on me to take her home. Dangling by my fingertips below her, I remembered we were in this together. Nitta and Tam, we were a team. Only then, somehow, did I manage to drag myself onto the bridge and collapse exhausted on the concrete span.

I allowed myself a minute or two to rest. It was fully light now. The sun had risen. Sitting next to Nissa, my arms wrapped around her, I watched Big Barry rocking out into the waves beyond the river mouth. For as far as I could see, the sea was brown and discoloured by the floodwater. Trees, branches and rubbish floated out almost as far as the horizon.

Finally, I took Nissa by the hand and we began walking very carefully along the railway sleepers towards the southern end of the bridge. I had never felt so tired in my life. Nor so elated. We had made it. I could hardly believe that we had faced so many obstacles, so much danger, yet we were alive, safe, and finally on our way home.

A whistle blew.

No way! protested my mind. *No way can that be a train!*

I was wrong.

24
TRAIN

The two hundred carriage iron-ore train came sweeping around the bend. Already it was rushing onto the bridge. The whistle blew again, a high frantic sound that said: 'Get out of the way! Get off the bridge! Jump into the river if you have to!'

I wasn't going to jump back into the river. Nissa and I had had enough of Crocodile River. Even as I lifted my little cousin up in a piggyback and began running awkwardly over the widely-spaced railway sleepers towards the nearer end of the bridge, I knew that the train, laden with twenty thousand tonnes of ore, would never be able to stop in time. I would never be able to out-run it. Still, I kept running.

The whistle shrilled again, much closer now. I couldn't look around. I concentrated on my feet, on placing them squarely on the narrow wooden sleepers, rather than in the ten-centimetre gaps between them. The entire bridge was shaking. There was a loud rumbling sound and the protesting shriek of metal on metal as the train driver applied the emergency brakes. The air seemed to throb in my ears. Nissa, bouncing on my back, was crying out about a crocodile. The train was just behind us now, almost on us! I could feel it, I could feel the wall of air it pushed ahead of it. It whistled again, so close that the sound was deafening. We were fifty metres from the end of the bridge now. Fifty metres from safety. It might as well have been fifty kilometres. We were never going to make it. My legs felt like lead, my lungs burned but still I kept running. And Nissa kept shouting about a crocodile. It made no sense, who cared about crocodiles now? Then a shadow fell over us, a strong wind nearly flattened me. Finally, I realised what Nissa was saying.

Mustering the last of my strength, I launched myself off the side of the bridge.

25
PROMISE

For a heart-stopping moment, Nissa and I hung in mid-air. Then, as the train hurtled past in a storm of sparks and smoke and diesel fumes, my outstretched right hand closed around the dangling rope.

Not crocodile, *Copter*. That's what Nissa had been shouting.

Sixty seconds later we were safely inside the helicopter. While the pilot put the aircraft on a course for Crocodile Bridge, his crewman helped us to our seats. *Seat*, actually, because Nissa refused to let go of me.

'I guess she'll be okay on your lap,' the crewman said, fastening the safety harness around us.

He fetched a couple of blankets and wrapped them around us, too.

'Would either of you like some chocolate?' he asked.

A silly question. It even drew a smile from Nissa.

As we pigged out on chocolate bars, the crewman explained how they had found us. At first light, a fisherman had come upon Nathan McDonald washed up on the beach near the mouth of Crocodile River. Our kidnapper was still alive! After he was swept away from the baobab, Nathan had grabbed hold of a passing log and managed to hang on all the way to the ocean. As they drove to the hospital, Nathan told the fisherman everything. The fisherman phoned the police and a helicopter was sent down the river looking for us. So Nathan was instrumental in saving our lives. I hoped the judge would take that into account when he went to trial.

'Tam?'

I looked down at Nissa. She had chocolate smeared all over her face. 'What is it, Niss?'

'Tam take Nitta home now?'

'You betcha,' I said, and this time it was a rock-solid promise.

About the author

Born in New Zealand, Justin D'Ath is one of twelve children. He came to Australia in 1971 to study for missionary priesthood. After three years, he left the seminary in the dead of night and spent two years roaming Australia on a motorbike. While doing that he began writing for motorbike magazines. He published his first novel for adults in 1989. This was followed by numerous award-winning short stories, also for adults. Justin has worked in a sugar mill, on a cattle station, in a mine, on an island, in a laboratory, built cars, picked fruit, driven forklifts and taught writing for twelve years. He wrote his first children's book in 1996. To date he has published fifteen books. He has two children, two grandchildren, and one dog.

www.justindath.com

ACTION HAS A NEW HERO. SAM FOX IS BACK!

BUSHFIRE RESCUE

OUT NOW

COMING SOON:

SHARK BAIT
SCORPION STING